JAN BRETT

COZY IN LOVE

putnam

G. P. PUTNAM'S SONS

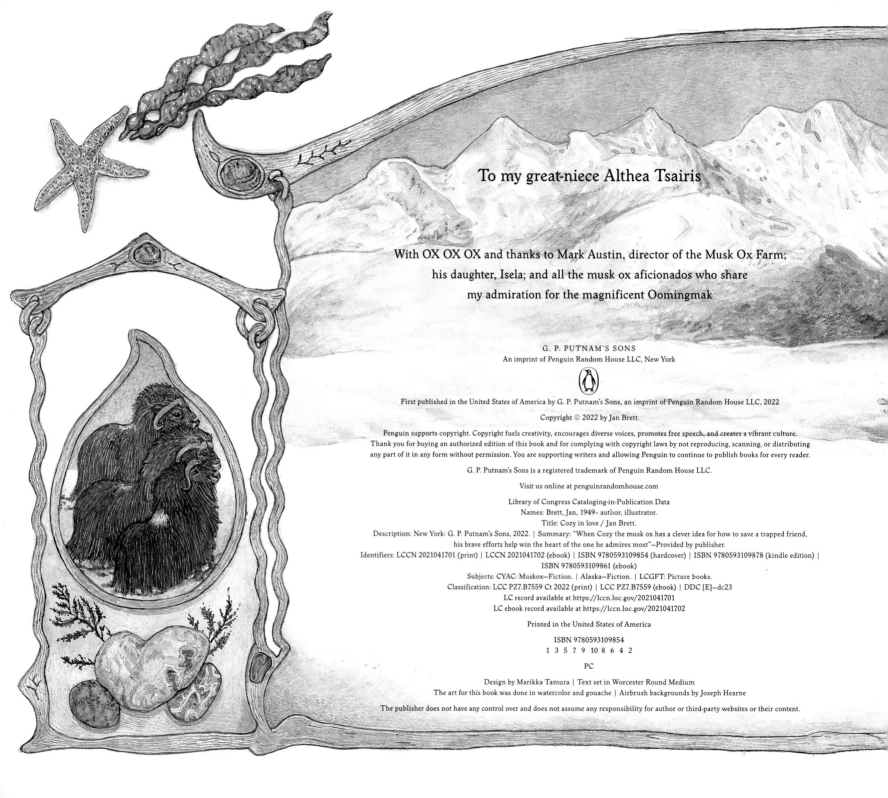

To my great-niece Althea Tsairis

With OX OX OX and thanks to Mark Austin, director of the Musk Ox Farm;
his daughter, Isela; and all the musk ox aficionados who share
my admiration for the magnificent Oomingmak

G. P. PUTNAM'S SONS
An imprint of Penguin Random House LLC, New York

First published in the United States of America by G. P. Putnam's Sons, an imprint of Penguin Random House LLC, 2022

Visit us online at penguinrandomhouse.com

Library of Congress Cataloging-in-Publication Data
Names: Brett, Jan, 1949– author, illustrator.
Title: Cozy in love / Jan Brett.
Description: New York: G. P. Putnam's Sons, 2022. | Summary: "When Cozy the musk ox has a clever idea for how to save a trapped friend,
his brave efforts help win the heart of the one he admires most"–Provided by publisher.
Identifiers: LCCN 2021041701 (print) | LCCN 2021041702 (ebook) | ISBN 9780593109854 (hardcover) | ISBN 9780593109878 (kindle edition) |
ISBN 9780593109861 (ebook)
Subjects: CYAC: Muskox–Fiction. | Alaska–Fiction. | LCGFT: Picture books.
Classification: LCC PZ7.B7559 Ct 2022 (print) | LCC PZ7.B7559 (ebook) | DDC [E]–dc23
LC record available at https://lccn.loc.gov/2021041701
LC ebook record available at https://lccn.loc.gov/2021041702

Printed in the United States of America

ISBN 9780593109854
1 3 5 7 9 10 8 6 4 2

PC

Design by Marikka Tamura | Text set in Worcester Round Medium
The art for this book was done in watercolor and gouache | Airbrush backgrounds by Joseph Hearne

*B*ish, *bash, BISH! Bish, bash, BOOM!* Every fall, the musk ox bulls
charged each other and bashed heads.

"I am strong!" snorted one.

"I am stronger!" bellowed another.

It was the musk ox way. Each one wanted the attention of the herd.

Cozy was catching his breath after a heartbreaking loss. He sought
the admiration of lovely Lofti. She had a sparkle in her eye that set her apart.
He hoped she could see that under his massive coat, there was a caring heart.

Left behind, he buried his aching head in the Alaskan snow.

He didn't hear the whirring of wings.

Plop. A small fish landed on his nose, and his eyes popped open. It was his puffin friend with a frantic plea for help.

"Cozy!" Puffin called. "I flew over Teardrop Inlet. Young Bella is still playing around in there. Air is getting cold. Ice will trap her!"

Cozy leaped to his hooves, heart pounding.

Bella was a beluga whale. She loved to play in Teardrop Inlet.

Her whistles and chirps sounded like silver bells.

She splashed with her flukes and made rainbows. The nearby puffins would topple off their perches with laughter when she paraded by with seaweed on her head.

But Teardrop Inlet was a dangerous place during freeze-up.

Even when she was a baby, her mother had warned her:

"When the sea freezes, the entrance gets closed off.
It is not called Teardrop just for its shape. It is also for the
tears shed when one of our pod gets locked in."

Sure enough, when Cozy slid to a stop above the inlet, Bella was singing songs and splashing rainbows, totally distracted from the ice forming.

One last turn under the waterfall, thought Bella, and then I'll go.

But when she tried to head out to sea, she was stopped by steely-gray ice.

"Oh no!" Bella squeaked from her icy pool.

"Oh no!" called Puffin from above.

"Oh no!" groaned Cozy.

Bella tried to heave herself over the ice, which had hardened like rock.
She threw herself as high as she could, but she couldn't reach freedom.
It wouldn't be long before the calm water in the inlet froze over,
leaving Bella no way to reach the air.

Not far away, the musk ox herd was bedding down for the night, with grown-ups on the outside, big horns showing strength, and youngsters safe in the middle.

But curious Lofti drifted off to follow Cozy.

Cozy looked down at the tiny inlet. Then, with a huge rumble, a big chunk of glacial ice fell and splashed into the water.

For a moment, he thought the wave might be big enough to help push Bella to freedom.

"Go, Bella!" screeched Puffin, Cozy, and Lofti.

But Bella did not make it over the ice wall. *I have to save Bella,* Cozy thought. *I must think of a way.*

Puffin landed on one of the nearby boulders carried down by the glacier. The big rock gave Cozy an idea.

Simple science, he thought. Heavy rocks could take up room.
The water just might rise to a new level.

Maybe all that head bumping could serve
a new purpose.

He took a running charge, lowered his massive
horn boss, and puuuuushed!

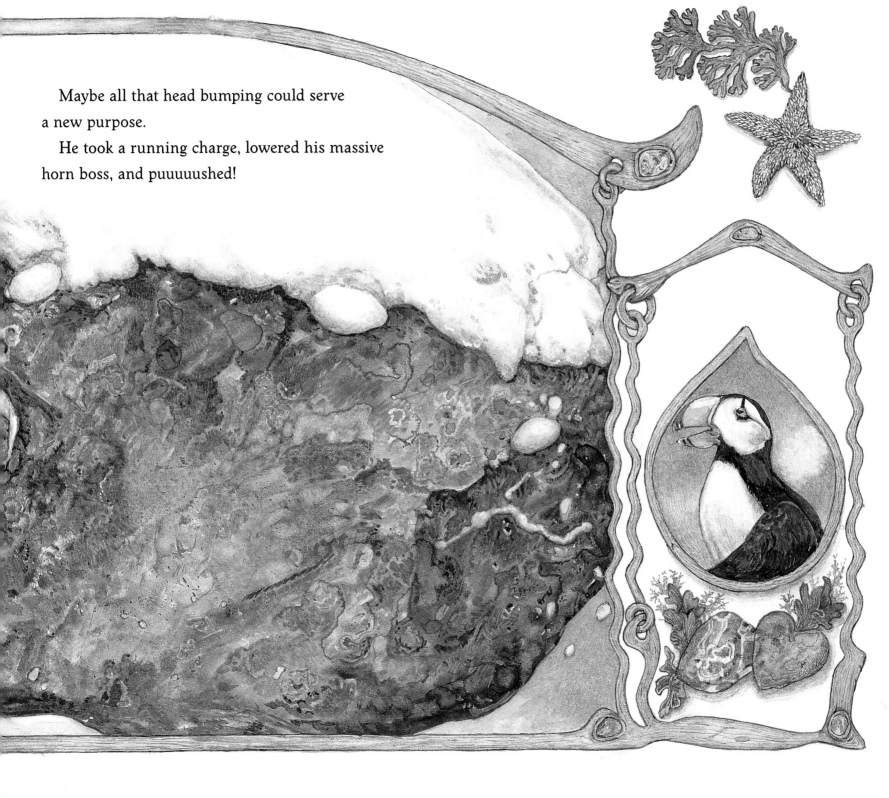

Crash! The boulder landed with a tremendous splash.

Puffin got the picture.

"Look out below!" he called.

Bish! Cozy bumped another huge boulder. *Bash!*

A giant piece of mountain was next to go.

Bish, bash, crash! Bish, bash, crash!
Cozy didn't stop until boulders filled the inlet to brimming and
Bella rode the crest of a rolling wave into the deep Bering Sea.

Cozy panted, and his poor head ached. He sat down in the tussocks and rested on a pillow of snow.

Then Cozy was enveloped by silky-soft musk ox qiviut, the coziest, woolliest fur on earth.

He turned to see the warm brown eyes of his admiring friend.
Lofti had watched the whole thing. She knew a strong, smart,
bighearted ox when she saw one.

"Musk ox in love," commented Puffin.

"Musk ox in love,"
whistled Bella,
dancing in the sea.

Cozy and Lofti did not have to say a word. They watched the pod of
belugas become smaller and smaller pale dots beneath the sea.

Then, keeping steady with musk ox ways, Cozy and Lofti headed back
to their herd, muzzle to muzzle.